For Sue

PHILOMEL BOOKS

A division of Penguin Young Readers Group. Published by The Penguin Group. Penguin Group (USA) Inc., 375 Hudson Street, New York, NY 10014, U.S.A.
Penguin Group (Canada), 90 Eglinton Avenue East, Suite 700, Toronto, Ontario M4P 2Y3, Canada (a division of Pearson Penguin Canada Inc.). Penguin Books Ltd, 80 Strand, London WC2R ORL, England.
Penguin Ireland, 25 St. Stephen's Green, Dublin 2, Ireland (a division of Penguin Books Ltd). Penguin Group (Australia), 250 Camberwell Road, Camberwell, Victoria 3124, Australia (a division of Pearson Australia Group Pty
Ltd). Penguin Books India Pvt Ltd, 11 Community Centre, Panchsheel Park, New Delhi – 110 017, India. Penguin Group (NZ), 67 Apollo Drive, Rosedale, North Shore 0632, New Zealand
(a division of Pearson New Zealand Ltd). Penguin Books (South Africa) (Pty) Ltd, 24 Sturdee Avenue, Rosebank, Johannesburg 2196, South Africa.
Penguin Books Ltd, Registered Offices: 80 Strand, London WC2R ORL, England.

Manufactured in China. The art for Up and Down is made entirely of watercolour (that's right, with a U) on Arches cold-pressed paper. Except for the writing. That was done in pencil.

Library of Congress Cataloging-in-Publication Data
Jeffers, Oliver. Up and down / Oliver Jeffers.—1st ed. p. cm. Sequel to: Lost and found.
Summary: Even though the penguin and the boy are close friends and do many things together, the penguin decides that he wants to fly and he wants to do it on his own.
[1. Penguins—Fiction. 2. Flight—Fiction. 3. Friendship—Fiction.] I. Title. PZ7.J3643Up 2010 [E]—dc22 2010011358
ISBN 978-0-399-25545-8
1 3 5 7 9 10 8 6 4 2

Up and Down

This WAY →

OLIVER JEFFERS

PHILOMEL BOOKS • AN IMPRINT OF PENGUIN GROUP (USA) INC.

Once there were two friends . . .

who always did
everything together.

Until the day the penguin decided there was something important he wanted to do by himself . . .

...fly!

He did own wings, after all,

although they didn't seem to work very well.

But that didn't stop the penguin from trying.

Nothing worked,
and it wasn't long before
he began to run out of ideas.

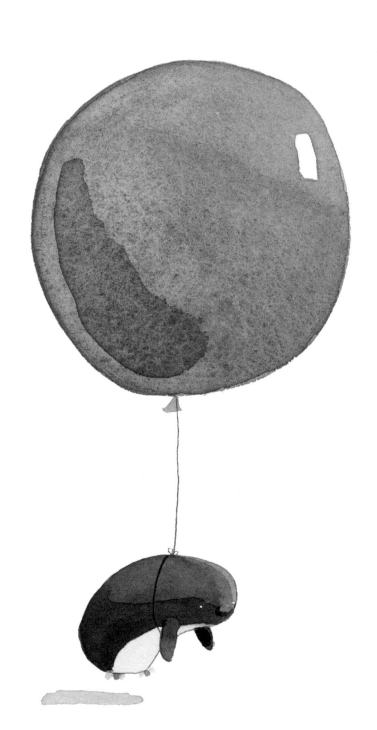

The boy even offered him a
ride in his plane, but it wasn't the same.

The penguin wanted to do this by himself.

After doing a bit of homework,
it seemed like the odds were
against him . . .

and together they decided
it was time to ask for help.

Before they could ask, something caught the penguin's eye and he knew this was his chance.

In his
excitement,
he rushed off
without a word.

And the boy didn't know
where he had gone.

He looked everywhere,
and even thought he'd
found him for
a second . . .

but none of
these penguins knew
how to play his favorite game.

Meanwhile, the penguin had found
the right place and was hired on the spot.

Finally he'd get to fly.

Suddenly he realized
he didn't know
where the boy was . . .

or how to get home.

Later that night, when the penguin should have been excited, he couldn't help but miss his friend.

Likewise, the boy
could barely sleep
for worrying
about *his* friend.

The next day, the boy tried to think
of all the places the penguin might go,

when something caught his eye.
He didn't have much time.

The penguin's moment had come,
but suddenly he wasn't sure about flying anymore.

He wished the boy were there.
Had his friend even noticed he was missing?

But it was too late for thoughts like that.

He took off like a bullet.

The boy rushed in hoping he could still
catch his friend.

The penguin couldn't believe how high or fast he was going, and he had no idea how he was going to land.

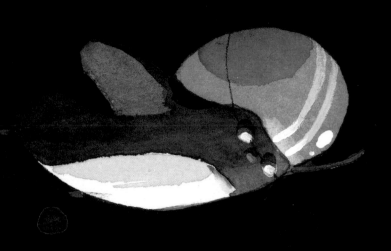

He was terrified and
missed the boy more than ever.

The boy was there to catch him.

The friends agreed that there was
a reason why his wings didn't
work very well...

because penguins don't like flying.

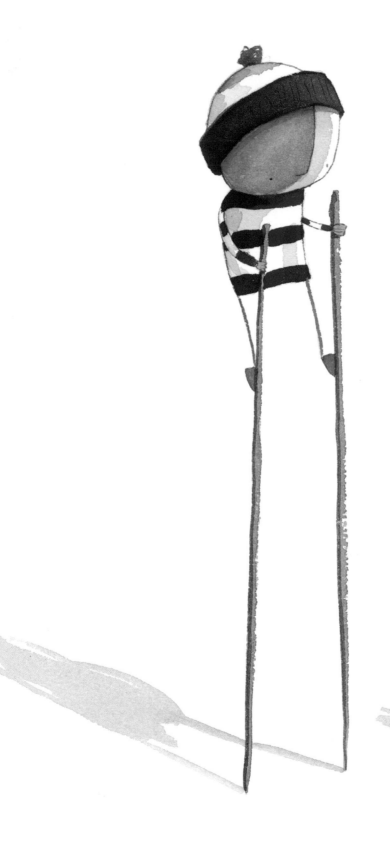

The two friends
made a break
for home . . .

to play their favorite game.